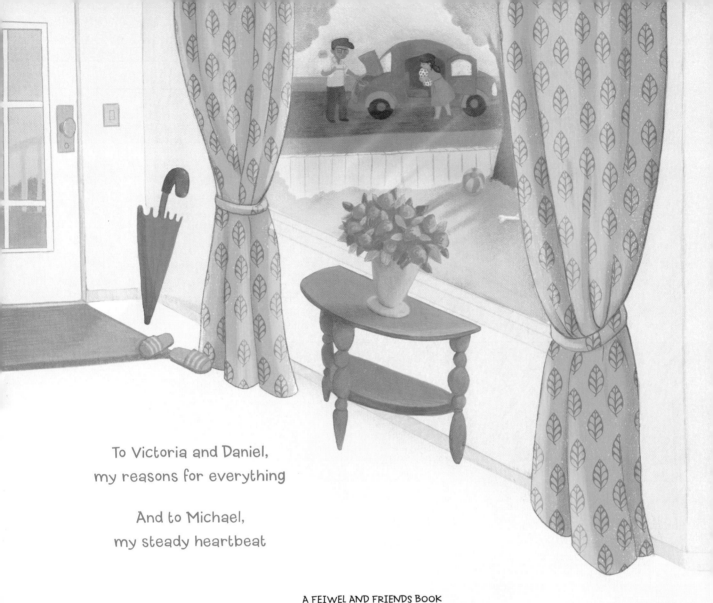

To Victoria and Daniel,
my reasons for everything

And to Michael,
my steady heartbeat

A FEIWEL AND FRIENDS BOOK
An imprint of Macmillan Publishing Group, LLC
120 Broadway, New York, NY 10271 • mackids.com

Copyright © 2023 by Olga Herrera. All rights reserved.

Our books may be purchased in bulk for promotional, educational, or business use. Please
contact your local bookseller or the Macmillan Corporate and Premium Sales Department
at (800) 221-7945 ext. 5442 or by email at MacmillanSpecialMarkets@macmillan.com.

Library of Congress Control Number: 2022910007

First edition, 2023
Book design by Mina Chung and Naomi Silverio
This artwork was created using Procreate on an iPad.
Feiwel and Friends logo designed by Filomena Tuosto
Printed in China by RR Donnelley Asia Printing Solutions Ltd.,
Dongguan City, Guangdong Province

ISBN 978-1-250-82767-8 (hardcover)
1 3 5 7 9 10 8 6 4 2

THE UNWELCOME SURPRISE

OLGA
HERRERA

Feiwel and Friends · New York

Bongo's day always began the same:

He would roll out of bed,

greet Sister as she
watered his potted plant,

scratch his back on
his favorite chair,

and take a delicious whiff of his stinky carpet on his
way to the kitchen, where Mom served him breakfast.

Until one morning . . .

WHOA!

A bizarre new thing
interrupted the trip
to his plant.

A bunch of weird new things smothered his favorite chair!

And something new kept Mom from serving him breakfast!

Bongo tried to ignore the changes that were creeping into his day.

A whiff of his favorite stinky carpet would make it all okay.

His family gathered around all these strange new things.

What was happening?

Was his family changing?

Oh no!

What if . . .

That monstrous new thing eats all his food?

Or he never reaches his plant again!

And his poor chair! It would
definitely be squashed!

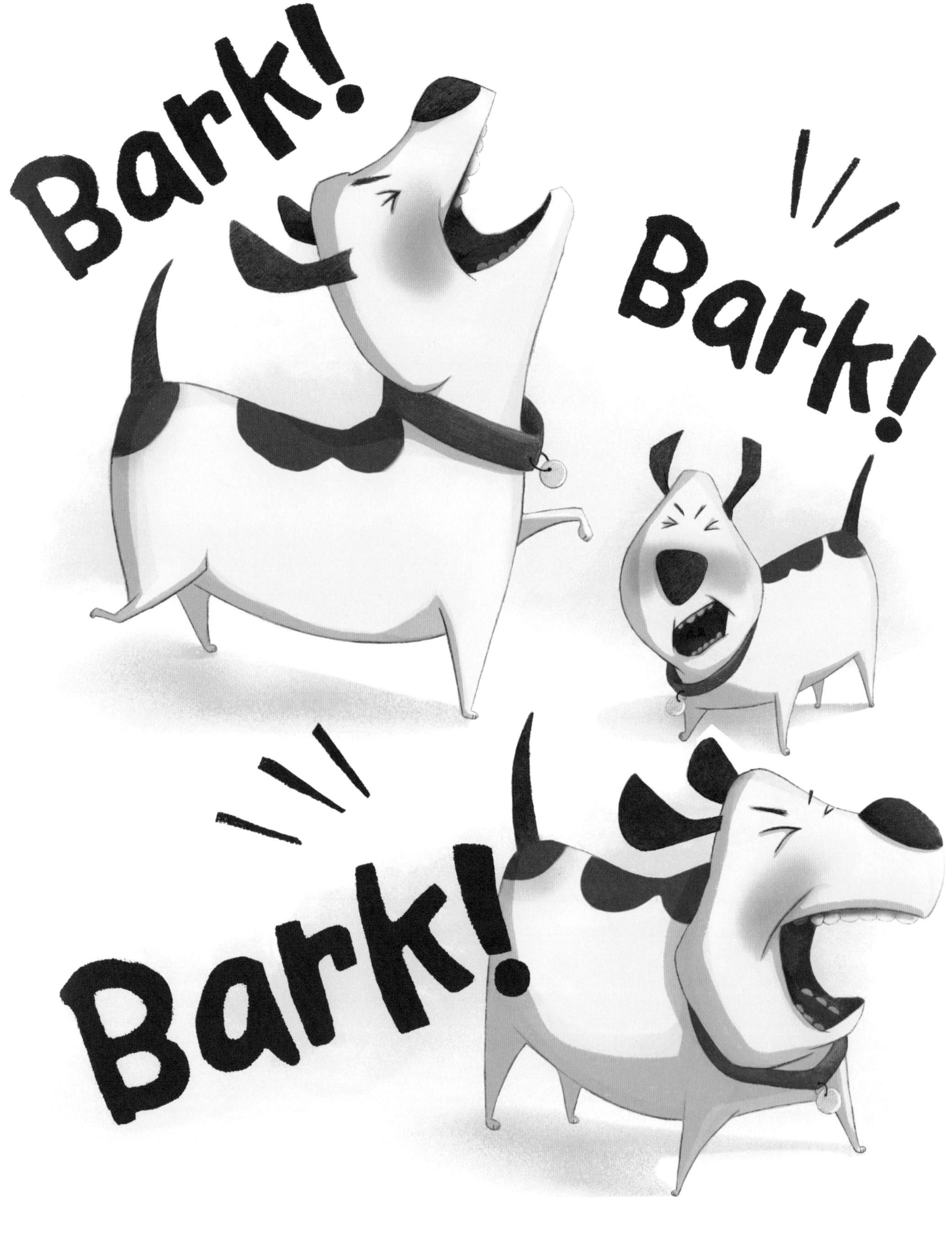
Bark!
Bark!
Bark!

He had to take those things off his chair!

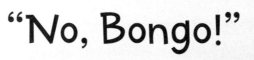

"No, Bongo!"

There were strange new things all over his house.

Mom hadn't fed him yet.

He was shushed by Sister

and now scolded by Dad!

His family wasn't acting as usual.
Nothing was okay!

Finally, he did the only thing a respectable dog
could in this situation . . .

That was the last straw.
He was sent to TIME OUT.

What were all those annoying new things for?

And his plant! It didn't look right in that corner!

What about his stinky carpet . . . Would it smell different?

His tummy was not feeling well.

Luckily, at that moment . . .

Mom called him for breakfast. "Here you go, Bongo!
We'll be starting our day a little later from now on," she said.

But Bongo was too worried to eat his
food. He eyed the sneaky new thing
creeping around the corner.

He rolled one perfectly round
morsel of food toward it.

The sneaky thing didn't eat it.

After breakfast, Dad called him over.
"Come here, Bongo. We have a surprise!"

Bongo liked surprises, but all those new things
were too close to his chair.

Dad helped him out.

Nothing was normal. But things were . . . okay?
Nothing that Bongo had imagined had actually happened!

Just as he was settling down . . .
Something new filled the room.

It was **HORRIBLE**.

It was **LOUD**.

Waaaah!

It was . . .

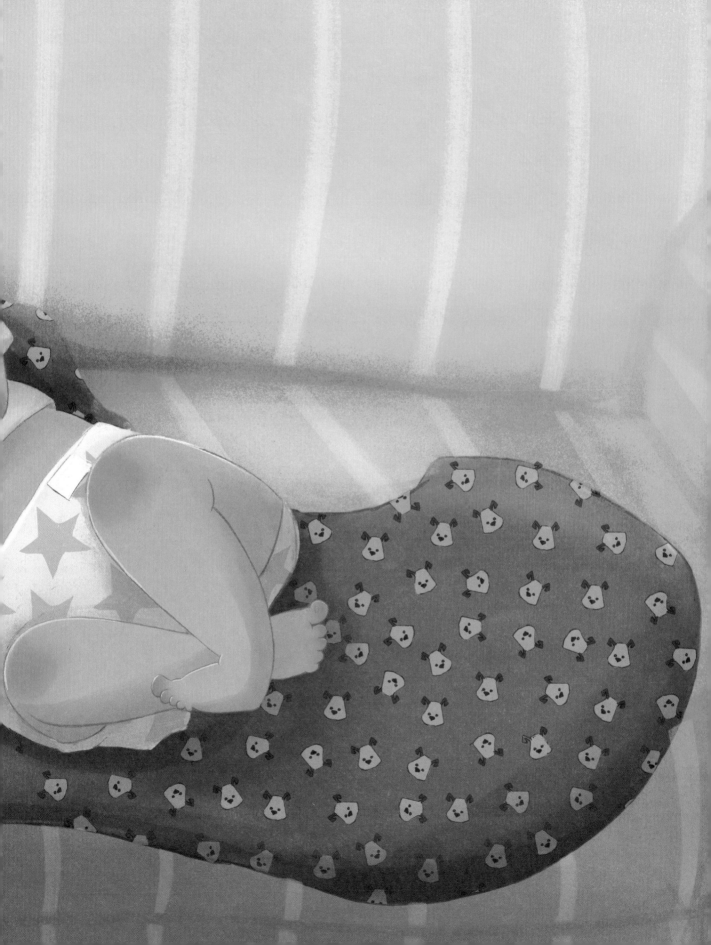

Bongo looked . . . and wondered.

Bongo sniffed . . .
    and liked.

Bongo touched . . .
    and loved.

The next morning, Bongo got out of bed in his cozy new room,

greeted Sister watering his plant in a perfect new spot,

scratched his back on his
fun new thing,

and rolled on his old chair,
where Dad had cleared a spot
just for him!

Bongo headed to the kitchen, where Mom
fed him breakfast and added a special treat!

And after breakfast, Bongo went to take a whiff of . . .

His favorite new thing.

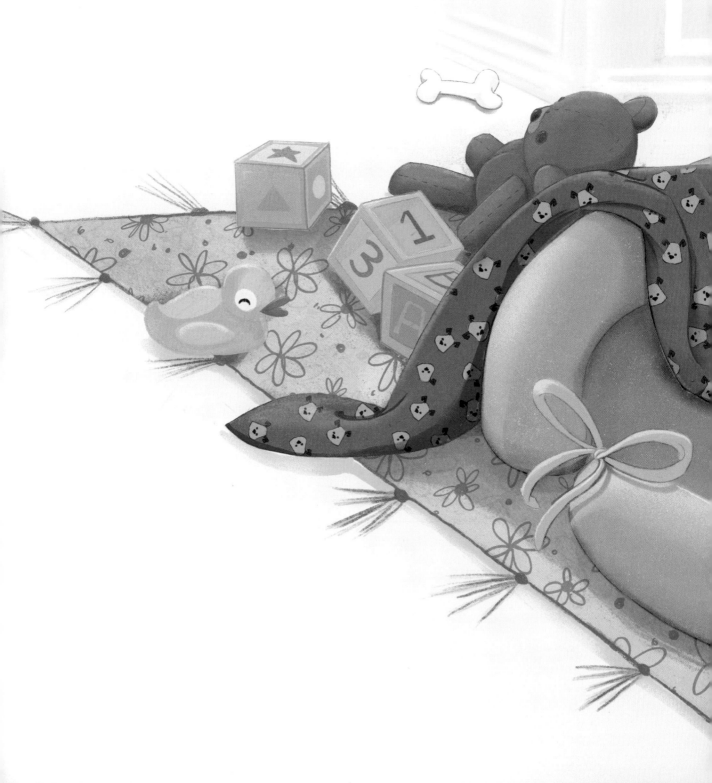